Will and Wisdom

what about Perseverance?

Copyright ©2016 by Will and Wisdom Books

Illustration copyright ©2016 by David Riley

Art Direction and Design: David Riley Associates, Newport Beach, California Rileydra.com

Published in 2016 by Will and Wisdom Books, Newport Beach, California
and BluSky Publishers, Franklin, Tennessee

ISBN 978-0-9970531-3-5

This book belongs to

....

It was the first day of soccer

practice and *Will* was very excited,

until he heard the coach say, "I want

to see what kind of shape you guys are

in, so we are going to start practice by

running a mile."

Will admitted to *Wisdom*, "I don't think I can run a mile." "Sure you can," encouraged *Wisdom*. The coach told everyone to get on line, then he looked at his stopwatch and blew his whistle.

Everyone started to run. They had

to run four laps around the track to

equal one mile. After the first lap, the

coach yelled, "Pick it up boys!" *Will*

said to *Wisdom*, "I'm not going to be

able to make it."

"What do you mean?" questioned

Wisdom. "You can make it. It's all about

perseverance." "Per-se-what?" asked *Will.*

"Perseverance," repeated *Wisdom.*

"It means to keep going when things get

tough, to never give up." *Will* decided to

keep on running.

After the second lap, the coach yelled,

"Come on boys, my grandmother can run

faster than you!" *Wisdom* poked his head

out of *Will's* backpack and said, "The coach's

Grandmother sounds like an amazing athlete.

Maybe she should play on the team."

Will started to laugh, "Don't make me laugh, *Wisdom*. I'm trying to run." "Oh, sorry," apologized *Wisdom*. "I've got a pain in my side and it's getting worse. Do you think I should stop?" *Will* asked. "Keep going," *Wisdom* said. "But what about the pain?" asked Will. "You can handle it," replied *Wisdom*.

Just past the half-mile point, three boys stopped

and dropped out of the run. Then, just before the

start of the final lap, two more boys gave up. Sweat

was pouring off of *Will's* head and his legs felt

like they weighed one hundred pounds each. But

he kept going. The last lap would be the hardest.

"I'm really tired *Wisdom*," gasped *Will*.

"I'll tell you what," *Wisdom* said, "You just keep going, putting one foot in front of the other and I'll tell you why perseverance is important. When I'm finished, if you still want to stop, then you can stop. OK?" That sounded reasonable to *Will*, so he agreed.

Wisdom began, "The Bible is full of

stories about people who could have taken

the easy way out and stopped or given up,

but we see that their perseverance was

used by God to accomplish great things.

When things got hard and they were wondering where God was, they just kept going. God is pleased when we trust Him and finish what we begin. Does that make sense?" "It does," admitted *Will*.

The pain in his side didn't go away and his legs still felt really heavy but *Will* kept going and finished the run. The coach was really proud of all of the boys who finished. The boys who didn't finish were told that they had to run a mile at the next practice. *Will* was happy that he kept going and didn't give up.

THE END

Because you know that the

testing of your faith develops

perseverance. Perseverance must finish

its work so that you may be mature and

complete, not lacking anything.

James 1:3-4

A Prayer To Follow God
and Become a Christian

Dear God,

Help me to be strong and never give up. I believe
you love me so much that you gave your only Son,
Jesus, to die on the cross for the things that I have
done wrong. Please forgive me and come into my
life and change me. I believe that Jesus rose from
the dead and is coming back some day. Until then,
I will follow you for the rest of my life. Jesus is my
God, my Savior and my forever Friend. In Jesus'
Name, Amen.

_____   _____

your name   date

If you have just prayed that prayer and meant it with all your heart, you are a child of God and will live with Him forever in heaven.

Here's what you can do now:

1. Read the Bible to learn more about God.

2. Go to church and worship with other believers.

3. Be baptized so that others know of your commitment to follow God.

4. Pray everyday and thank the Lord for all that you have.

5. Know that you can do and accomplish anything with God in your life.